High Mountains

Starlight Caves

Rainbow Pools

Huts

Ice Owls

Burning Bushes

Lake

Sledging Slopes

Kennels

Gardens

School

Ridge

LAND OF ICE AND WINTER

Husky Training Ground

Fields

Linda Chapman lives in Leicestershire with her family and two dogs. When she is not writing, she spends her time looking after her three children, reading, talking to people about writing, and horse riding whenever she can.

You can find out more about Linda on her websites at *lindachapman.co.uk* and *lindachapmanauthor.co.uk*

Books by Linda Chapman

BRIGHT LIGHTS
CENTRE STAGE
MY SECRET UNICORN series
NOT QUITE A MERMAID series
SKATING SCHOOL series
SKY HORSES series
STARDUST series
UNICORN SCHOOL series

Skating
Violet Skate Friends
School

Linda Chapman

Illustrated by Nellie Ryan

PUFFIN

Madame Letsworth's Magic Ice-Skating Academy

FROST FAIRIES

MOLLY HANNAH EMILY TILDA ALICE

ICE OWLS

AMANDA   ZOE   HEATHER   TASHA   OLIVIA

SNOW FOXES

CAMILLA   TESS   CLARE   HELENA

To Michele and Jessica Holland for all the great ice-skating advice and for reading the books. Thank you! Any mistakes are most definitely mine.

PUFFIN BOOKS

Published by the Penguin Group
Penguin Books Ltd, 80 Strand, London WC2R ORL, England
Penguin Group (USA) Inc., 375 Hudson Street, New York, New York 10014, USA
Penguin Group (Canada), 90 Eglinton Avenue East, Suite 700, Toronto, Ontario, Canada M4P 2Y3
(a division of Pearson Penguin Canada Inc.)
Penguin Ireland, 25 St Stephen's Green, Dublin 2, Ireland (a division of Penguin Books Ltd)
Penguin Group (Australia), 250 Camberwell Road, Camberwell, Victoria 3124, Australia
(a division of Pearson Australia Group Pty Ltd)
Penguin Books India Pvt Ltd, 11 Community Centre, Panchsheel Park, New Delhi – 110 017, India
Penguin Group (NZ), 67 Apollo Drive, Rosedale, North Shore 0632, New Zealand
(a division of Pearson New Zealand Ltd)
Penguin Books (South Africa) (Pty) Ltd, 24 Sturdee Avenue, Rosebank, Johannesburg 2196, South Africa

Penguin Books Ltd, Registered Offices: 80 Strand, London WC2R ORL, England

puffinbooks.com

First published 2010
2

Text copyright © Linda Chapman, 2010
Illustrations copyright © Nellie Ryan, 2010
All rights reserved

The moral right of the author and illustrator has been asserted

Set in Bembo MT 15/22pt
Typeset by Palimpsest Book Production Limited, Grangemouth, Stirlingshire
Made and printed in England by Clays Ltd, St Ives plc

British Library Cataloguing in Publication Data
A CIP catalogue record for this book is available from the British Library

ISBN: 978-0-141-32634-4

www.greenpenguin.co.uk

Mixed Sources
Product group from well-managed forests and other controlled sources
www.fsc.org Cert no. SA-COC-1592
© 1996 Forest Stewardship Council

Penguin Books is committed to a sustainable future for our business, our readers and our planet. The book in your hands is made from paper certified by the Forest Stewardship Council.

Contents

In the Magic Land of Ice and Winter...

Everything looked just as it always did. A blanket of crisp snow covered the fields and meadows, towns and villages. Frozen lakes glittered in the rays of the sun and a mist hung over the tops of the jagged mountains. Silvery robins darted from tree to tree while white fluffy fox cubs tumbled after each other. But the

ice sylphs who lived in the land knew
something was different.

One of the mountains in the land had
changed shape. Something had curled
around it, great wings folded flat. Its
dark-red scaly sides moved in and out,
and steam from its huge nostrils formed
thick clouds, melting the snow and ice all
around.

Madame Letsworth, the
headteacher of the Magic
Ice-skating Academy,
stared anxiously out of her
study window. She knew
that the ice sylphs did not
have long.

In the gardens below
her, fourteen human girls
ran about, throwing

snowballs, chattering and dragging sledges around. Madame Letsworth gazed down at them. She hoped that one of them would be able to help the magic land – the one who would be chosen to be the Ice Princess.

Her forehead furrowed. The question was: which one would it be?

Chapter One
Best Friends

'Are you ready?' Molly called.

Emily sat down on her sledge and
pushed strands of her shoulder-length
chestnut-brown hair into her fleece hat.
'Yep!'

'Hannah?' asked Molly.

'Just a minute.' Hannah carefully got
her sledge into position on the other side
of Emily and began to tuck the ends of

her scarf neatly into her coat collar. Her long blonde hair was pulled back into a tidy single plait.

Emily's blue eyes swept over the glittering snowy slope. On the far side of the snow-covered lawn there was a grey stone building with icicles hanging from its window ledges. Happiness fizzed through her. The Magic Ice-skating Academy. A week ago, Emily had been whisked out of her normal human life and had arrived on a frozen lake just outside the school in the magic Land of Ice and Winter. At first, she had thought she was dreaming, but she had quickly found out that it was real!

Emily could vividly remember standing with all the other girls in the school hall on that first day, listening to Madame

Letsworth, their headteacher, telling
them that if they wanted to, they could
stay at the ice-skating school for six
weeks to learn about the land and
improve their skating. At the end of that
time, one of them would be chosen to be
the land's Ice Princess, a girl who would
help the ice sylphs in some way. Madame
Letsworth hadn't said how the girl would
help, but she had told them that if the Ice
Princess was successful, she would be
granted a wish.

After finding out that no time would
pass in the human world and no one
would miss her at home, Emily had
immediately decided to stay. The
thought of being in a magical land,
skating every day, making friends and
living in a boarding school where there

were all sorts of other fun wintry things
to do like sledging and cross-country
skiing seemed almost too good to be
true.

Emily had been at the school for a
week now and, although she missed her
family a bit, being in the Land of Ice and
Winter was brilliant fun. One of the best
things about it so far had been making
friends with Hannah and Molly.

'OK, I'm almost ready,' called Hannah.
'But are you sure this is safe, Molly? We

might crash into a tree or a bush, and the slope's quite steep.'

'It'll be fine,' said Molly airily.

'You know, maybe we should start a bit further down,' Hannah said anxiously. 'It really would be safer and . . .'

'No, no, no,' Molly interrupted, her dark eyes gleaming. 'OK. So the person who goes furthest wins!'

'But . . .' Hannah protested.

Molly ignored her. 'On your marks . . . get set . . . *go!*' she yelled.

Emily pushed off. All three sledges started slowly, but within seconds they were gathering speed, bumping over the surface, going faster and faster as they headed down the hill towards the garden. Seeing a holly bush coming up, Emily tried to steer round it, pulling as hard as

8

she could on the rope, but she was too late! The sledge's front-runners caught the branches of the bush and it stopped with a jerk.

'Whoa!' Emily yelled as she was thrown off into the snow. She scrambled to her feet laughing. Her coat and gloves were covered in snow crystals, her face was wet and cold, but she didn't care. She looked round and saw that Hannah had fallen off too. Hannah's hat was lying in the snow, but she was grinning. 'Well done. You beat me, Em!'

Molly had reached the bottom. Seeing the other two stuck up the slope, she whooped. 'I won! I won! *Losers!*'

Emily grabbed a handful of snow. She ran down the slope, hurling it at Molly. Hannah giggled and joined in. Molly shrieked and started to throw snowballs back. When they finally stopped, they were covered with even more snow, but their eyes were shining and their cheeks were flushed.

The school bell rang out, signalling the end of lunchtime.

'Come on,' Hannah said eagerly. 'It's skating class. We don't want to be late.'

Pulling their sledges behind them, they hurried across the gardens and back into the school.

The ice rink where the girls had their skating classes was one of Emily's favourite places. It was down a long corridor and had a domed glass roof through which you could see the sky and, at night-time, the stars. Three times a day, hundreds of tiny frost fairies swept over it, smoothing the ice so that it was perfect to skate on.

The frost fairies kept everything in order at the school. They organized the students' clothes, kept the building clean and tidy, and prepared all the food. They had glittering gauzy wings and clouds of fluffy hair, and they chattered to each other in high-pitched voices, which none of the girls could understand. Emily loved them and they seemed to like her too. Three of them came to land on her shoulder now as she walked to the lockers at the side of the rink.

Each girl had her own locker where she kept her skates and several layers of clothing in case she got cold.

As Emily, Molly and Hannah laced up

their boots, they were joined by Tilda and Alice from their dorm. Tilda was slim with dark skin and black hair. Alice was small, and she had pale skin, blonde hair and a round friendly face.

'Hi there,' Tilda said, plonking herself down on the bench beside them. 'What have you lot been doing?'

'We went sledging. It was brilliant,' said Hannah. 'How about you?'

'We went to the kennels to see the husky puppies,' Tilda replied.

'They're gorgeous!' enthused Alice.

'You think every animal is gorgeous,' Molly teased. 'I bet you even think stick insects are gorgeous.'

Alice grinned. 'I do actually. I've got ten of them back at home.'

'And two gerbils, a guinea pig, two cats, a dog and a hedgehog who lives outside but who you feed,' Emily put in. She'd heard all about Alice's pets. In fact, she knew all about her friends' home lives now. In the last week they'd done a lot of talking!

She had learnt that Tilda was a star gymnast and had two brothers and two sisters and that Hannah was an only child who had been skating since she was three

and was determined to be an Olympic
ice-skater one day. Molly had only
started skating a few years ago, but had
turned out to be really talented at it and
she now had lessons with a private coach.
She had an older brother and a goldfish
called Scooby Doo.

Emily looked round at her four friends;
they were all so different, but the great
thing was that they all got on really well.
Last week, she had been in the Snow
Foxes dorm, but she hadn't really made
friends with any of the other girls there,
and she had been really pleased when
Madame Letsworth had let her move
into the Frost Fairies dorm instead.

Hannah got up. 'Come on, let's start
warming up.'

They headed on to the ice. 'Do you

think we'll find out what the competition is going to be this week?' Molly said.

'And what colour skates the winner will get?' added Tilda.

Emily felt a rush of excitement. Even though she was one of the least experienced skaters in the school, she had won the very first competition the day before. It had been to skate a routine showing that you were skating from your heart. Winning it – and being presented with the beautiful snow-white skates that had been the prize – had been one of the best moments of her life.

'I wonder what the competition will be,' Hannah said.

Emily hugged herself. She couldn't wait to find out!

Chapter Two
The Announcement

A pretty girl with long dark hair and a red dress was standing by the entrance to the rink stretching one leg up on the bench and talking loudly to anyone who would listen.

'I did a triple toe loop followed by a Flying Camel this morning. Madame Letsworth was here and she said it was the best she'd seen since we all started.'

Amanda smiled smugly as she talked
about the ice-skating jumps she'd done.
'But then that's not surprising; after all, I
have been skating for longer than nearly
everyone else here . . .'

'I wish a Flying Camel would land on
Amanda's head,' Molly muttered to Emily,
who giggled. Amanda was one of the
most annoying girls at the school! She was
always boasting and bossing people about.

Emily got on well with most of the
other girls. There was only one person
she didn't like at all – Camilla.

When they had first arrived, Emily and
Camilla had both been in the Snow Foxes
dorm. But when Emily had started going
round with Hannah and Molly, who were
in one of the other dorms, Camilla had
declared that Emily wasn't allowed to be

friends with them too and had started being mean to her. It hadn't helped that Emily had then won the competition at the end of the week, after Camilla had told everyone *she* was bound to win.

Emily glanced at the rink. Camilla was skating in the centre of the ice, gliding round on one leg. Emily started some warm-up stretches. She did a lot of ballet at home and so she was very flexible, which really helped with her skating.

First she stretched down to touch her toes, the palms of her hands easily reaching the ice. Then she straightened up and put her foot on the barrier around the rink, her leg straight.

Camilla skated past. 'Pity you can't skate as well as you can warm up, Emily,' she said snidely before skating off.

Emily took a deep breath and tried not to let Camilla's comment upset her. She *could* skate well. She'd proved it by winning the competition. She might not be as experienced as all the others, but she was trying hard and she knew she was improving every single day.

Emily set off round the rink, her arms out, her head held high. She went faster and faster and then added in some turns and jumps until the skating teachers arrived. Monsieur Carvallio was dark-skinned and tall. He taught the beginners' group that Emily and Tilda were in with a sweet but very shy girl called Heather. The intermediate skaters were taught by Madame Li and the advanced skaters had Madame Letsworth. Molly and Hannah, who were both in the advanced group, said she was the best skating coach they had ever had.

The three teachers skated on to the ice. Madame Letsworth, who was wearing a dark-maroon dress as usual, blew her whistle. 'Gather round, girls. Before we start, I'm going to tell you about this week's competition.'

'Cool!' said Molly, skating up at full speed to join Emily and stopping in a spray of ice crystals.

'However, first,' continued Madame
Letsworth, 'I have an important safety
announcement. If you are skating outside
on the lake behind the school, please
don't go down the small river that goes
into the woods to the east. The ice is
weak and there is a big crack in it. The
other rivers are all fine. Now, for the
competition . . .'

Madame Letsworth looked round at
the girls' eager faces. 'This week we

would like to see how well you skate together with another person and so your challenge will be to produce a two-minute routine in pairs that tells a story. You must choose the music and story in your pairs. We want to see how well you all get on, working as a team.'

Wow! That sounded fun! Emily exchanged excited looks with Molly.

Zoe, who was in the Ice Owls dorm, put up her hand. 'Do we get to choose our own partners, Madame?'

To Emily's disappointment, Madame Letsworth shook her head. 'We have drawn your names out of a hat and put you in pairs. I will tell you who you will be skating with after this lesson.'

'What colour skates will the winners get this week?' asked Tilda.

'The winning pair will each be presented with their own special pair of violet skates. Now, time to get started,' Madame Letsworth said. 'Let's not waste any more ice time.'

And the lesson began.

Emily had been practising lots. She could now do jumps and spins, although nothing like as complicated as the ones that the girls in the advanced group did, but it was wonderful to be able to whizz round on the spot and fly over the surface of the ice.

She glided on one foot in a spiral, one leg in the air, her arms and head arched back.

'Well done, Emily,' Monsieur Carvallio praised her.

Emily lowered her leg and skated on, glowing with happiness. She wondered who would be her partner in the competition and if they would be good enough to win. She loved the thought of having violet skates as well as her special white ones.

As Monsieur Carvallio turned his attention to Tilda, Emily looked round at the others. Everyone on the rink was concentrating hard, working on their own or with a teacher.

It's funny how everyone's skating is so different, Emily reflected as she watched them all. Tilda was really daring on the ice and ended up falling over all the time because she was forever trying jumps and spins, almost seeming to forget she was on the ice. Alice, who was in the

intermediate group, was laid-back and
never seemed to get upset about anything.
She skated effortlessly and didn't try too
hard or worry too much. Hannah was the
opposite. She took ice-skating very
seriously indeed. She always looked so
elegant and she practised extremely hard.
Amanda always skated as if she expected
the whole world to be watching her,

throwing her arms wide and skating dramatically, and Molly . . .

Emily grinned as she saw Molly skating really fast and throwing herself into a double salchow jump followed by a double toe loop, wobbling on the landing, but just about managing to stay on her feet. Molly did everything super-quickly on the ice, just like in real life. She was a ball of energy and was really exciting to watch.

I wonder what I'm like as a skater, Emily wondered. She had been told that she was very expressive. She hoped she was. She loved dancing on ice, feeling the music carrying her and being able to lose herself in it. Ballet was wonderful, but ice-skating was even better because she could go so fast and when she jumped she really felt like she was flying. Emily sighed happily. There was nothing better than skating!

'Come along, Emily,' called Monsieur Carvallio. 'Another spiral, please.'

Emily focused her attention on what she was supposed to be doing and glided off across the rink.

After the lesson, the girls changed out of their skating boots.

'Time to find out who we're going to be skating with in the competition,' Molly said excitedly as Madame Letsworth waited for them to gather round.

Emily felt a flicker of nerves. Who would she be with? Hannah or Molly, she hoped. But Alice or Tilda would be great too.

Madame Letsworth waited until they

were all changed and then looked down at her list. 'Here are the skating pairs for the competition. Hannah, you will be dancing with Alice.' Hannah and Alice exchanged delighted looks. 'Zoe, you will be with Heather. Molly, you will be dancing with Tilda.'

'*Yes!*' both Molly and Tilda said.

So who am I going to be with? Emily thought.

'Camilla with Olivia, Helena with Tess, Tasha with Clare . . .'

Emily tried to work out who hadn't had their name read out yet. She looked round, pairing them off. Oh, no, surely not . . .

Madame Letsworth smiled at her. 'And, Emily, you'll be with Amanda.'

Chapter Three
Partners

Emily's heart sank to her toes.

'But Emily's just a beginner!' Amanda
protested loudly. 'She can't skate
anything like as well as I can.'

'That is a matter of opinion, Amanda,'
said Madame Letsworth crisply. 'And
anyway, the competition will be judged
on how well you work as a team. Like last
week, the difficulty of the routine is not

important. This is about skating with your heart again, but doing so with a partner.'

Amanda pursed her lips. Madame Letsworth clapped her hands to drown the buzz of noise that had broken out as everyone started talking to their new partners.

'Tomorrow morning's lessons will change slightly because of the competition. You will be free to spend the morning with your partner, working out your routine. Good luck and remember to work *together!*'

She walked away.

Hannah and Molly turned to Emily. 'Oh, you poor, poor thing!' Molly breathed sympathetically. '*Amanda!*'

Camilla, who was standing nearby, snorted with laughter. Emily felt awful.

She'd have rather been with just about anyone else – well, apart from Camilla. That would have been even worse!

Tilda came over. 'I'm so glad I'm with you,' she said to Molly.

'We'll do an awesome routine,' agreed Molly.

Hannah caught Emily's eye. 'I'm sure being with Amanda will be OK, Em,' she said encouragingly.

Emily glanced over at Amanda, who was marching away from the rink looking cross. If only she felt so sure herself!

After their afternoon break, they had a lesson in the schoolroom with Madame Longley. Madame Longley taught them all about the Land of Ice and Winter. Over the last week she'd described some of the amazing creatures that inhabited the land – mountain lions that lived in caves, silver deer and snow foxes.

Emily usually loved Madame Longley's lessons in the high-ceilinged classroom with big windows that looked out over the snowy land. Today, however, she found it hard to concentrate. She kept glancing at Amanda as Madame Longley showed them pictures of the ice monsters who lived under the ice and looked like giant polar bears. Oh, why did she and Amanda have to be partners?

Her attention was caught though when the teacher brought an ice dragon into the classroom for them all to see. The ice dragon was tiny, only about the size of Emily's palm. His scales were a pale silvery-blue colour and he had leathery wings on his back. Emily had seen ice dragons before. They worked the music boxes that produced the music the girls danced to when they were on the ice. Emily loved them and often lifted the lids on the music boxes to say hello and tickle their heads.

'Oh, wow! He's so cute!' Alice exclaimed. 'Can we hold him?'

'Of course. Ice dragons are very

friendly.' Madame Longley passed him around. 'In the wild, they usually live in forests and have nests like birds. They are very sociable creatures and hate being on their own. They can also be quite mischievous at times!' When it was Emily's turn to hold him, the tiny dragon sat on her palm and looked up at her with big dark eyes as shiny as jewels. Then he snorted and a cloud of ice crystals shot out from his nostrils. Emily giggled.

Hannah looked at the teacher. 'It's weird. In our world, we don't have dragons, but there are stories about them and they are really big and breathe fire, not ice.'

'We do have fire dragons.' Emily saw Madame Longley's eyes flicker to the window. 'They fly around the edge of

our land, passing here on their way to
other places. They're gigantic,
unpredictable creatures, stubborn and not
very clever, although generally kindly.
Thankfully, they do not usually stop here
because their breath is very hot – it can
melt ice and snow, which can be very
dangerous in a land like this. It is almost
impossible to persuade them to move on

once they've landed and, if they go to sleep, they sleep for a hundred years.'

'I'd love to see a fire dragon!' enthused Molly, taking the little ice dragon.

'Me too!' said Tilda.

'Maybe one of you *will* get to meet a fire dragon one day,' Madame Longley replied.

Emily heard a strange note in the teacher's voice and frowned. What did she mean? Once again she saw Madame Longley's eyes flick to the window, but just then the little ice dragon turned a somersault on Molly's hand and everyone gasped and crowded round. He sat up and then blew out another blast of icy air at them. Everyone laughed.

After the ice dragon had been put back in his cage, they all drew pictures of him and made notes about the two types of dragon.

'Wasn't that a brilliant lesson?' Emily said as they all left the classroom to go to the hall for supper.

'Yeah – brilliantly dull,' sneered Camilla, who was passing. 'Only you could think a lesson like that was fun, Emily. All that stuff about ice monsters and dragons. I'd far rather be skating. It's just a waste of time!' And she walked off.

Hannah shook her head. 'Can you believe her?'

'She's mad,' commented Alice. 'I think it's amazing learning about all the creatures here.'

'Did you notice the way Madame Longley went a bit strange when she started talking about fire dragons?' said

Emily. 'What did she mean when she said, "Maybe one of you will get to meet a fire dragon one day"?' A thought had been pinging around in her brain ever since that moment and now she looked round at her friends. 'You don't think the Ice Princess has anything to do with a fire dragon, do you?'

They all stared at her.

'I hadn't thought of that,' said Hannah slowly.

'Madame Longley did sound a bit weird when she said it,' Tilda breathed. 'Maybe you're right, Emily. Maybe the person who is Ice Princess will get to meet a fire dragon!'

'But why?' said Molly.

They all exchanged uncertain looks.

'Oh, I hope we find out more soon,'

said Emily longingly. 'I want to know what the Ice Princess will have to do.'

'And I want to know how they're going to choose which one of us it will be,' said Hannah. 'Do you think it'll be the person who wins most of the competitions?'

'It must be something to do with the competitions,' said Tilda.

'In which case we'd all better practise loads,' said Molly.

Emily glanced across at Amanda, who was walking nearby, and her heart sank. She loved skating, but she wasn't looking forward to practising with Amanda at all!

At supper all everyone else in the Frost Fairies dorm talked about was their routines.

'Have you thought about what story you and Amanda are going to do?' Hannah asked Emily.

Emily shook her head. 'What about you?'

'We're going to do something about a toy coming to life,' Hannah said, looking at Alice.

'It'll be cool. Hannah's going to be the magician and I'll be the toy,' Alice said.

'Let's go and choose some music,' said Hannah. They got up from the table and hurried off.

Molly and Tilda went off together too. Emily saw Amanda heading out of the hall and went over to her. 'Hi,' she said.

Amanda looked at her. 'Oh, hi. I was going to come and talk to you. I've been thinking about the competition and I guess as long as you do what I tell you to and leave the planning of the routine up to me, maybe we'll do all right. Shall we meet straight after breakfast tomorrow in the music room and start then?'

'Oh, OK,' said Emily, taken aback by Amanda's bossiness.

Amanda gave her a brief nod and stalked off. Emily stared after her, her heart sinking. She wondered where she should go. She didn't feel like going up to the dorm on her own without the others and she didn't want to go to the common room where Amanda and Camilla would be.

I know, she decided, *I'll go to the rink.*

The ice rink was empty and silent apart from a group of frost fairies dusting the

benches with their tiny wings. Emily
laced up the special snow-white boots
with silver laces that she had won the
week before. She didn't like to wear
them for classes – it would have felt like
showing off because everyone else just
had plain white boots with white laces –
but she loved to wear them when she
was on her own like now.

The sky was black overhead and the
stars were twinkling. Stepping on to the
smooth ice, Emily began to skate round.
As she skated, she felt some of the
tension start to leave her – *push and glide,
push and glide*. She concentrated on her
steps, on keeping her chin high, her
shoulders down, her arms out to help her
balance. What did it matter about
Amanda and the competition? Emily

could still skate. She began to do some crossover steps and then looked round in surprise as music suddenly filled the air.

She saw one of the frost fairies fluttering beside the music box and a little ice dragon poking his head out from under the lid. The music that the dragon had put on was bouncy. Emily grinned – she couldn't resist. She started to skate in time to it.

The music got faster and Emily danced across the ice before jumping into the air, turning a single loop jump, her arms tight to her chest. For a moment she felt like she was flying. She landed perfectly with her arms out and skated on. The music built again. She propelled herself off her right foot, up into the air. Crossing her ankles together, she spun round, the stars shining above her. She wobbled slightly on landing, but didn't fall, and finished with the music, stopping with her arms above her head. She smiled.

Hearing the faint sound of clapping, she looked round. The frost fairies had all stopped their tidying to watch and were clapping their tiny hands, and the dragon was nodding and flapping his wings. Emily skated over and curtseyed.

'Thank you!' she grinned as the fairies rose up and fluttered round her face and shoulders like a cloud of glittering butterflies.

She meant it. The skating had made her feel so much better. It was as if all her worries and unhappiness had slipped from her into the ice, leaving her feeling happy again.

OK, Amanda's annoying, but so what? Emily thought. *I only have to be her partner for a week and I don't have to spend any time with her when we're not practising. I'm not going to let it get to me and I'm not going to moan. I've got all my other friends and that's the most important thing.*

Feeling much happier, she headed off the ice, got changed out of her skates and went up to her dorm.

Chapter Four

The First Practice

'No, Emily! You don't do it like that,'
Amanda said, putting her hands on her
hips and sighing. 'Your leg wasn't straight
enough. And you've got to keep your
chin up and stay centred. I've already told
you that!'

Emily took a deep breath. It was
halfway through the morning and
Amanda had been ordering her about

ever since they had met up after
breakfast. Emily was finding it very hard
to be as positive as she had been the
night before on the ice.

First Amanda had announced they were
going to perform a piece from the ballet
Swan Lake. Amanda was going to be the
beautiful enchanted princess who was a
swan in the daytime and a girl at
night-time, and Emily was going to be the
prince who almost shoots her when she is
a swan and then falls in love with her.

'If you're the prince then you don't
have to do any difficult skating,' Amanda
had said. 'You can just watch me and
skate around a bit.'

'But can't I do some spins and jumps?'
asked Emily.

'Well, maybe you could do one jump

and a spin,' Amanda huffed. 'You can do sit spins, can't you?'

Emily nodded.

'Well, I suppose we could work one of those in then, and maybe, just maybe, a single toe loop. I guess the prince could jump for love when he sees how beautifully I dance.' Amanda smoothed her hair. 'But what you'll really have to do is look at me most of the time.'

Oh, great, Emily thought. 'But . . .'

'Come on, let's go to the rink and get started,' Amanda interrupted bossily.

Amanda had skated through the beginning of the routine she had worked out and was now trying to show Emily what to do. 'Right, you circle round me while I do this.' Throwing back her arms, Amanda glided round

the ring like a swan before turning into
a layback spin and then skating on,
lifting one leg into the air and holding
her arms behind her.

Emily's eyes wandered round the rink.
Other people had come to practise too
and Madame Li and Madame Letsworth
were watching the girls from the side.
Hannah and Alice were doing jumps
together. On the far side of the ice,
Heather was working hard with Zoe.
They seemed to be really listening to each
other. Molly and Tilda were arguing
because they both kept changing the steps.

'No, Tilda,' Emily heard Molly saying. 'We said you'd do three crossovers, turn and skate backwards, not two crossovers and a single flip.'

'But I want to do a jump,' said Tilda mutinously. 'Why do we always have to do what you want, Molly?'

Amanda skated over. 'Emily, you're not watching! This is where you skate over and take my hands and we skate together and then split and spin round. Now, come on!'

Emily sighed and turned her attention back to her own routine.

'I don't know how you're managing to put up with Amanda,' said Hannah as she, Molly and Emily ate lunch together. After working so hard all morning, it was lovely to have big bowls of pasta and cheese and then apple crumble for pudding. The frost fairies fluttered around, clearing tables after the students and whisking away any mess.

'She's so bossy,' Molly said. 'And you don't seem to do much in your routine. She does all the skating.'

'I know,' said Emily. 'I wish I was with one of you.'

'Actually, I wish you were with me too,' sighed Molly. 'Tilda is a bit of a nightmare. She argues all the time and when we do agree something, she'll sometimes just go off and do something different because she feels like it.'

Emily hid her grin. Molly could be a bit like that too!

'Alice is OK,' sighed Hannah. 'She

doesn't argue, but she doesn't seem very keen on practising. I wanted to try again at lunchtime, but she said she wanted to go and see the husky puppies.'

'I'm sure she'll start practising more in the next few days,' said Emily, trying to make Hannah feel better. 'We did have a long session this morning.'

'We could go and look at the puppies too,' Molly suggested. 'I'd like to see them.'

'Me too,' agreed Emily.

So, after lunch, they headed to the kennels where the huskies lived. The huskies pulled sledges across the snow so that people could travel if they weren't skating or skiing. They looked just like huskies from the real world, but here their coats were flecked with silver, and, when they ran across the snow and ice, rainbow-coloured sparks shot out from their claws.

When the girls walked into the kennels, the puppies came bounding over. Alice and Tilda were there already. 'Hi there!' Tilda called. 'What do you think of the puppies?'

'They're gorgeous!' Molly said, picking one up and cuddling it.

Alice sighed happily. 'I wish I could spend every minute here. This one is

Snowflake, this one is Frisky, this is Max, this is Prince and this is Rosie.' She pointed out the different puppies. Within seconds, Emily had forgotten which was which, but she didn't care. She cuddled them all.

After a while, Molly got bored and suggested they went sledging again.

'I'd rather go skating,' said Emily.

'Well, how about we go skating outside?' suggested Molly.

'OK,' Emily agreed. She loved skating outside on the rivers. Hannah nodded too.

'I'm going to stay here,' said Alice.

Tilda said she would too, so Emily, Hannah and Molly went to fetch their skates. At the back of the school there was a frozen lake with three big rivers and some small rivers running down to it from the mountains in the distance.

'We'd better not go down there,' said Hannah, pointing to a small river to the east that led between overhanging trees.

'That's the river where Madame Letsworth said there was a crack, isn't it?' said Emily.

Molly nodded. 'Let's go down the main West River instead.'

They set off. It was wonderful to be skating outside. The cold air stung Emily's cheeks, but she didn't care. The sky was cornflower blue overhead and, on the bank at the side, a family of white fox cubs were playing. In the distance, she could see the misty mountains rising dramatically up into the sky. 'I'd love to go and explore more,' she said longingly. 'This land's so amazing.'

'Me too,' agreed Molly. 'It would be

brilliant to see all the creatures that
Madame Longley keeps telling us about.'

'Like ice monsters and mountain lions,'
agreed Emily. 'Maybe we'll get to go out
into the land more in the next few
weeks.' She rolled her eyes. 'I'd far rather
do that than practise for this competition
with Amanda.'

'It's only for five more days,' Hannah
told her. 'Then you won't have to be
with Amanda any more.'

'I guess,' Emily sighed.

Molly darted forwards. 'Look, let's not
talk about it now. Let's play tag.' She
touched Emily's shoulder. 'You're on, Em!'
She and Hannah quickly skated away.

Pushing all thoughts of the competition
and Amanda out of her head, Emily
laughed and skated after her friends.

Chapter Five
Falling Out

The next few days flew by. Most people were taking the competition very seriously. Whenever there was any spare time, the ice rink was busy with people practising and everyone's tempers started to fray as the competition drew closer.

'Emily, you're not looking like a prince!' Amanda said on Friday morning as they practised before breakfast. 'We're never going to win if you don't skate better than that.'

'But all I'm doing is skating in a circle and it's boring,' Emily protested. 'Maybe I should do some more jumps. It would make me feel more prince-like.'

'No,' said Amanda. 'You'd only mess up and fall over. And please make sure you look as if you're in love with me!'

Emily gave her an exasperated look, but Amanda was already skating off to practise the part of the routine where she changed from a swan into a girl. Emily sighed and glanced round. Hannah was skating on her own. 'Where's Alice?' called Emily.

'Gone to the kennels again.' Hannah frowned. 'She only practised for ten minutes. It's so irritating! I'm going in. There's no point practising on my own.'

thought. *It's just her luck to be with a partner who doesn't want to practise.* She heard raised voices and looked round. Molly and Tilda were arguing again.

'We've got to stick to what we've agreed, Tilda!' Molly was saying angrily.

'Oh, stop being so bossy!' said Tilda. 'Just because you've been skating longer than me doesn't mean you should make all the decisions.'

'I'm not trying to make all the

decisions!' Molly exclaimed. 'I just want us to agree on what we're doing, otherwise we're going to look rubbish. You're being really annoying, Tilda!'

'Look who's talking!' Tilda snapped back and she skated away.

'Well!' Molly stared after her, hands on hips, her face like thunder.

Just then, Amanda called across the ice. 'Emily! Come on!'

Emily skated to join in, but she was so busy thinking about Molly that she found it hard to concentrate. As she prepared herself for her jump, one of her skate blades caught an edge on the ice, her arms windmilled and she banged down heavily. She gasped as the impact made the breath leave her body.

Molly came skating over. 'Are you all

right?' she asked anxiously, offering Emily a hand up.

Emily nodded. It had been a hard fall, but, although she felt shaken up, she was OK.

Amanda arrived. 'That was so dumb, Emily! I can't believe that you've only got one jump to do and you messed it up. I hope you're not going to do something like that in the competition. We'll look like total idiots if you do and –'

'Amanda!' Molly interrupted angrily. 'Don't you think you should be asking Emily if she's OK and not having a go at her? She's just fallen over! Why do you always have to be so mean?'

'Molly, leave it,' sighed Emily. She could see Molly's temper was still up following her row with Tilda.

'I'm not mean,' Amanda protested.

'You so are!' Molly retorted. 'All you do is boss Emily about. If she wasn't so nice, she'd tell you to get lost.'

Madame Li came skating over. 'Is everything all right, girls?'

'Yes, fine, Madame,' Amanda said quickly. She smiled sweetly at the teacher. 'Emily fell and Molly and I just came over to see if she was OK.'

Molly and Emily exchanged glances.

'Are you all right, Emily?' Madame Li asked.

Emily nodded. 'Yes, thank you, Madame.'

'Good. It's just about time for everyone to come in anyway.' Madame Li raised a whistle to her lips and blew a long blast, a signal that it was time for the girls to clear the ice.

Amanda glanced at Emily. For a moment Emily thought she was about to say something, but then she turned and skated off the rink.

'I don't know how you put up with her!' said Molly. 'I'm going to get her back for being so nasty to you.'

'How?' Emily exclaimed.

Molly looked thoughtful. 'I don't know, but I bet I'll think of a way.'

★

For the rest of the lessons that morning, Molly and Tilda ignored each other. Hannah was hardly talking to Alice, but Alice didn't seem to notice. She was very worried because one of the husky puppies had gone missing. He had wandered off when the puppies had been out having a run around in the gardens. Alice said that the ice sylphs who looked after the dogs had been out searching for him, but as yet no one had found him.

'Poor Prince will be freezing cold,' Emily heard Alice whispering anxiously to Tilda in ballet class before lunch. They all took ballet to help with their skating. 'He'll be really scared. Oh, I wish I could go and help look for him instead of doing lessons.'

'We'll go at lunchtime and look then,' Tilda said.

Hannah turned. 'You can't go and look for him, Alice. You promised me we'd practise.'

'But this is more important, Hannah!' protested Alice.

Hannah frowned. 'Don't you care that we've got a competition in two days?'

'It's just a competition?' said Alice.

Hannah looked as if she couldn't believe her ears. 'Just a competition?' she echoed.

Alice nodded. 'Yes, and even if Molly's right and the person who does best in all the competitions is going to be the Ice Princess, well, so what? I'd like to be chosen, but if I'm not, I'm not. It's far more important that we find the puppy.'

'But we have to do our best, Alice!'

Hannah's voice rose. 'We have to try and win!'

Emily saw Madame Breshnev, the ballet teacher, looking over and hastily shushed them all before they got into trouble.

As they reluctantly fell silent, Emily could tell from Hannah's face that she was cross with Alice. Alice didn't look too happy with Hannah either. Emily bit her lip. It was awful having everyone arguing. She just wanted all her friends to get on.

★

'I've got it!' Molly breathed as she, Emily and Hannah walked to lunch together.

'Got what?' said Emily.

'A trick to play on Amanda to get her back for being so horrible to you,' Molly said.

'Molly, you can't play a trick on Amanda,' Hannah said, looking worried. 'What if you get into trouble with the teachers?'

'I won't,' said Molly. 'I'll need your help though.'

'What is the trick?' asked Emily uncertainly. She liked tricks, but only if they weren't mean.

'Not telling.' Molly's eyes twinkled mischievously. 'You'll just have to wait and see!'

Chapter Six
Tricked!

Molly wouldn't say a word more about her planned trick, but after lunch she started organizing them. 'I need Hannah to come with me. And, Emily, in about quarter of an hour, you have to find Amanda and bring her to the gym changing room.'

'But how?' demanded Emily.

Molly waved a hand. 'You'll think of a way. Hannah, you come with me.'

'But . . .' Hannah protested weakly.

'Come on!' Molly, her eyes shining excitedly, grabbed Hannah's arm and dragged her away.

After ten minutes, Emily went over to Amanda.

'I've won loads of skating competitions back at home,' Amanda was saying loudly to Olivia and Tasha, who were in the Ice Owls dorm with her. None of them noticed Emily. 'You should see my trophies. My mum keeps them in a big cabinet on the wall.' She sighed. 'I'd do so much better in this competition with someone who wasn't a beginner like Emily. I mean, she falls over on the simplest jump.'

Emily swallowed and tried not to feel too hurt. She spoke loudly, pretending

she hadn't heard the comment. 'Oh, hi,
Amanda.'

Amanda jumped guiltily and looked
round.

'I was just wondering if you'd come to
the gym changing room with me. I
thought we could run through a few of
the steps I'm unsure of before gym – and
I was also wondering if you could help
me with my arabesques off the ice. I'm
having real trouble with them.'

For a moment Emily thought she
would say no, but then Amanda nodded.
'I suppose I'd better help you.'

They set off for the gym.

'So, what's the trouble you're having
with arabesques?' Amanda asked.

'Oh, just how high to get my leg,' said
Emily, inventing wildly. 'You're so good

at that. I thought you might be able to help.' Amanda looked pleased.

As they came through the changing-room door, Emily stopped dead. Molly and Hannah were lying on their backs on the changing-room benches with their eyes closed. They were circling felt-tip pens – with the lids on – around their eyes, pressing the tops against their skin.

'What are you doing?' Amanda exclaimed.

Emily was wondering the same thing!

'It's a special type of relaxing thing called pen-therapy,' said Molly, opening her eyes. 'Madame Li told me about it at lunch today. You use the end of a pen to press round your eyes and, as it goes over these areas called pressure points, you start to feel really relaxed. Madame Li told me everyone knows about it in this land and they do it before skating because it helps them focus and concentrate. Hannah and I thought we'd have a go.'

Amanda looked a bit disbelieving.

'You should try it,' Molly said. 'You'll try too, won't you, Emily?'

From the look in Molly's eyes it was clear she was meant to say yes. Emily nodded. 'Um . . . sure,' she said,

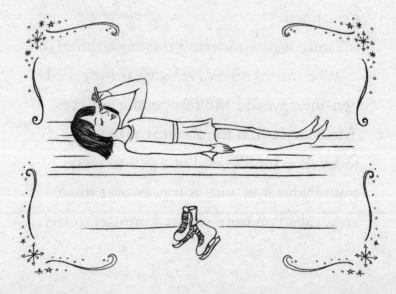

wondering what on earth Molly was doing.

'How about it, Amanda?' said Molly. 'Surely, if it makes your skating better, it's worth a try, isn't it? After all, if it doesn't work, it doesn't work. You've got nothing to lose.'

'I suppose so,' said Amanda. 'OK, I'll try it.'

Molly handed Emily a felt-tip pen. 'Make sure you keep the lid on,' she said with a grin. 'After all, you wouldn't want to get pen on your face.'

Emily lay down on the bench and started to circle the pen round her eyes.

'How does it feel?' Molly asked her.

'Um . . . OK,' Emily said hesitantly. She still didn't have a clue what Molly was up to.

Amanda lay down too. Molly picked up
a dark-blue felt-tip pen and passed it to her.

Amanda started running the pen in
circles around her eyes. 'That's it,' Molly
encouraged. 'Press quite hard, Amanda.'

Emily heard Hannah catch her breath
and sat up.

Everywhere Amanda moved the pen, a
trail of felt tip appeared on her skin. The
lid was on the pen, but, even so, it was
still drawing blue smudgy lines on
Amanda's face. There were now two
circles round her eyes where she had
been circling the pen. It looked like she
had drawn glasses on her face!

Emily's eyes shot to Molly. Her
shoulders were shaking and she was
clearly trying not to laugh. How had she
done it? The lid was on the pen!

Amanda frowned. 'It's not doing anything.'

'Oh, it is,' Molly grinned. She shrugged as Amanda looked at her. 'Maybe it doesn't work for you. Madame Li said it doesn't work for everyone.'

'It's stupid,' said Amanda. She stood up and put the pen down. 'I'm going to warm up for gym. Are you coming, Emily?'

'Yeah, in a minute.'

Amanda quickly marched out of the changing room and into the studio.

As soon as the door closed behind her, Emily, Molly and Hannah exploded with laughter.

'Oh, Molly! She looks so funny!' gasped Hannah.

'How did you do it?' Emily said.

Molly drew in her breath. 'Easy. I just

coloured over the end of the pen with another blue felt tip. It had dried by the time she picked it up and put it on her face, but it still comes off on skin. My brother did the same trick on me once.'

'She looked just like she'd been drawing on her face!' said Hannah.

'It's going to be so funny when everyone sees her!' said Molly.

Emily bit her lip. 'We have to tell her before then. Everyone will laugh and she won't know why.'

'Duh! That's the idea!' said Molly.

'But that's a bit mean,' said Emily.

'No, it's not,' said Molly. She saw Emily's face. 'She deserves it. She's been really horrible to you.'

'She does kind of deserve it,' Hannah said.

'No.' Emily shook her head. It felt OK for the three of them to have played a joke on Amanda, but it wasn't OK if it was going to make everyone laugh at her when she didn't know what was going on.

'I'm going to tell her,' she said.

'You can't!' exclaimed Molly. 'That would ruin the joke.'

'I don't care,' Emily said.

'Emily's right,' said Hannah reluctantly. 'We really should tell her.'

Molly looked cross. 'You two are so boring. Don't tell her, Emily.' Emily started walking towards the door. 'Don't!'

Emily knew Molly would be mad with her, but she had to tell Amanda. She pushed the door open, wondering what Amanda would say.

★

'What?' Amanda snapped out as Emily
explained. 'Molly played a trick on me?
I've got pen on my face?'

'Yes. It was just a joke,' Emily said
quickly as Amanda hurried through the
door and up to the mirrors in the gym
changing room.

'I can't believe you told her!' Molly
said crossly to Emily.

Amanda gasped as she saw her face.
She swung round.

'It was just a joke, Amanda,' Hannah said, almost apologetically.

Screwing up her face, Amanda looked like she was searching for words. An angry '*Grrrrr*' was all she could manage in the end. She turned to the sink and started hurriedly washing the pen off with soap and water.

'I hate you, Molly!' Amanda cried. Turning, she hurried back into the gym and slammed the door behind her.

Molly looked at Emily. 'Why did you have to tell her?'

'I just had to,' said Emily. 'How would you have liked it?'

'But I'm not annoying like her!' Molly snorted crossly and turned away.

Chapter Seven
The Crack in the Ice

Amanda ignored the three of them all
through gym and afterwards when they
had a cross-country skiing lesson. It
wasn't a fun afternoon. Molly was now
not speaking to Emily as well as not
speaking to Tilda. Alice and Hannah
were barely talking, and Alice was clearly
still worried about Prince. She spent a lot
of time staring distractedly into space.

'Alice, come on!' exclaimed Hannah crossly. They were having a relay race in two teams and she was captain of Alice's team.

Alice glared at her and stomped into position.

Emily was so busy worrying about them that she didn't hear Camilla, her team captain, calling her. Suddenly she felt a ski pole whack into her legs. She swung round. It was Camilla. 'Into the line – now!' Camilla snapped.

As captain, Camilla seemed to love having the chance to boss Emily around.

Emily bit back her angry reply and got into the line, her legs smarting. She was in the line behind Molly, who for a moment looked as though she was about to say something sympathetic and then seemed to remember she wasn't talking to Emily so looked pointedly away.

By the end of the lesson, Emily wanted nothing more than to get away from everyone. She slipped off and got her skates, warm coat, gloves and hat. Then she headed back outside. As she took in a deep breath of the fresh, crisp air and skated away from the school on the river, she felt a huge weight drop from her shoulders. Everyone was getting so cross with each other at the moment, it was a relief to be on her own.

I wish we could all just get on better, she

thought unhappily. She skated along the river, her boots gliding across the ice, left and right, left and right. As she lost herself in the regular rhythm, she felt all the tension inside her melt away. She was skating again and that was all that mattered. *And it really is all that matters,* Emily realized. *We shouldn't be falling out like we are doing just because of a competition. We all love skating and that's the main thing. It's stupid to argue.*

She jumped into the air, landing
perfectly on one leg. It was a brilliant
feeling to be able to whizz over the ice
like that and Emily knew that the only
people who really understood the feeling
were her friends at the Magic Ice-skating
Academy. It was so stupid to fall out over
a competition and silly things like tricks.

She sighed. Could she make the others
see it like that? It didn't seem likely.

Emily turned and headed back to the
school. As she got closer, she saw a few
other people heading off on their own
along different rivers or skating on the
lake behind the school. It seemed like
she wasn't the only one who had had
the idea of clearing her thoughts by
skating outside before supper. She saw
Molly, Hannah and Tilda all skating

separately and then, as she reached the
school, she caught sight of Amanda too.

Emily looked away. The one person
she was sure wasn't going to make up
and be friends was Amanda, but, to her
surprise, Amanda saw her and waved.

'Emily, can I talk to you?' she called.
Emily looked at her warily.

Amanda stopped in front of her. 'I . . .'
she hesitated. 'I wanted to say thank you
for telling me about the trick.'

Emily was so shocked she almost fell
over. Amanda blushed. 'Molly obviously

didn't want you to, but it would have been horrible if everyone had seen.'

Emily nodded. 'That's what I thought.'

Amanda looked at the ice. 'It was really nice of you. Look, I'm sorry if I've been a bit bossy. I didn't realize I'd been mean. It's just I really want to win.' She bit her lip. 'I'm not surprised Molly played a trick on me. I have been a bit horrible to you, haven't I?'

'Well, maybe a bit,' said Emily, still astonished but also feeling a sudden new liking for Amanda. 'But it's OK. I know you just want to win – I'd like to win too.' She thought about what she'd just realized out on the ice. 'It's not just about winning. We've got to enjoy it as well and do our best –'

She broke off as she caught sight of

someone skating slowly along the river they weren't supposed to go on. 'Look!'

Amanda followed her gaze. The person seemed to be searching the riverbanks. 'That looks like Alice.'

'It is Alice,' Emily realized. 'I bet she's looking for Prince, but she shouldn't be going down that river. Do you remember what Madame Letsworth said? There's a big crack in it.'

'We'd better stop her then,' said Amanda in alarm.

They began to skate quickly towards Alice, but by the time they had reached the narrow river, she had skated round a bend in the distance. 'Come on!' urged Amanda.

They skated even faster. As they rounded the bend, they saw Alice ahead of them, peering at the bushes. Emily gasped. She could see a large crack in the ice ahead, but Alice was so busy looking around she didn't seem to have noticed.

'Alice!' Emily shouted. 'Look out!'

But even as she shouted, there was a snapping noise and the weakened ice in front of Alice suddenly split open.

Alice cried out in alarm. She lost her balance and fell over just in front of the gap in the ice. For a moment Emily thought everything was going to be OK, but then the crack in front of Alice began to widen almost as if the ice on either side of it was being pushed apart by invisible hands. *Not invisible*, Emily realized with a massive shock.

Two hairy paws were gripping the edges of the ice, forcing the gap wider. There was an enormous roar and a white bear-like creature burst out of the water!

'Oh, no!' gasped Emily. 'It's an ice monster!'

Chapter Eight
Teamwork

The monster, who looked just like the ice monsters in the pictures Madame Longley had shown them in their lesson earlier in the week, hauled itself out of the water. As it did so, the ice Alice was sprawled on cracked. She screamed as she plunged into the freezing water below.

Amanda shrieked in horror.

Emily didn't hesitate. 'Get help!' she yelled. Amanda didn't move. 'Go on!'

Amanda turned and started skating back to the school as fast as she could. Emily raced frantically towards the gaping hole of water where Alice was splashing, unable to get out.

Emily's heart pounded. Her one thought was to pull Alice out. Hearing the ice creak worryingly beneath her, she threw herself down on her tummy. It

would be no good if she fell in herself!
She pushed herself towards the edge of
the ice, trying to ignore the great white
bear-like monster who was clambering
out of the water on to the nearby bank,
his coat dripping. If she could just get
Alice out then maybe they could skate
off before he got them. 'Alice! I'm here!'
She reached out as far as she could. Alice
flailed about in the water, trying to grab
her hands.

'Help me, Emily!'

The monster roared and then gathered
himself as if he was about to spring from
the bank into the water.

'No!' yelled Emily.

'Don't worry!' Alice gasped. 'He's –'

Her voice was drowned out by the
sound of voices and shouts behind them

and sticks came flying through the air
towards the ice monster.

'Leave them alone!'

'Get away from them!'

Emily glanced round and saw Molly,
Hannah and Tilda skating down the river
towards them. They threw sticks at the
bear, who drew back with a growl.

'Careful! The ice is too weak to skate
on!' Emily shouted.

'Don't worry!'

'We'll help you!'

'Hang on!'

Molly flung herself down on the ice,
wriggled over to Emily and grabbed her
feet. Emily realized Hannah was doing
the same to Molly. They hung on to her
in a big chain so she could lie down full
length and reach Alice.

'Alice! Here!' Emily shouted, edging closer on her tummy to the gap in the ice; Tilda grabbed more sticks from the bank and threw them at the bear to keep him away.

'Don't hurt him!' Alice gasped through chattering teeth. Her face was very pale. She tried to grab Emily's hands, but fell back into the water. Emily tried to edge out further, but the ice cracked around her and she had to pull back.

Just then, the monster reared up on his hind legs. All the girls apart from Alice screamed as he dived into the water.

Hannah and Molly threw themselves alongside Emily and frantically tried to grab Alice's hands.

He's going to get Alice! Emily thought.

And the bear did! He dived down and

came up again from underneath Alice,
pushing her upwards on his back. She
clung to his fur.

'He's . . . he's rescuing her!' Hannah
gasped as the bear swam to the bank and
clambered out. He stopped and Alice
scrambled down from his back on to the
safety of the riverbank. She was wet
through and shivering hard. 'Thank you!'
she gasped to him.

The other girls watched
open-mouthed as the monster sat down
beside her and licked her face with a
large pink tongue.

Alice looked up and saw their
astonished faces. 'He's friendly,' she
said. 'Ice monsters always are. Don't
you remember Madame Longley
saying it in class?' She stroked the giant
bear as if he was a big dog. He nuzzled
her.

'We thought you were in real danger!'
said Molly as they carefully skated over to
the bank.

'I was, but not from him,' said Alice.
'I could have drowned in the icy water.
Thank you for coming to save me.'

'We heard the screams,' said Tilda. She
went closer and cautiously stroked the

monster, who looked at her with black eyes and made a rumbling noise deep in his throat, almost like a cat purring.

'Why did you come down this river?' Hannah asked.

'I thought Prince might be here,' said Alice. 'I was so busy looking, I forgot about the crack in the ice.'

Emily hugged her. 'I'm so glad you're OK.'

'It was really brave of you to try and reach me,' said Alice, shivering.

'You'd have done the same for one of us,' Tilda told her.

Emily looked round at them all, remembering what she had been thinking before it all happened. 'We've been really stupid, arguing and stuff. I know the competition's important, but being friends is more important. We shouldn't be falling out because of it.'

Hannah nodded. 'You're right. It was so horrible seeing you in the water, Alice. I'm sorry for getting cross with you about not practising.'

'I'm sorry for not taking the practising more seriously and upsetting you,' Alice said.

Molly looked at Tilda. 'I'm sorry too.'

'And me,' said Tilda.

Hannah looked at Emily. 'You're the only one of us who really had reason to be cross with your partner and you've been really good about not arguing with her.'

'Where is Amanda anyway?' said Alice. 'I saw her with you when I fell into the water.'

'She didn't just skate off, did she?' Molly said indignantly.

'No, she went to get help,' said Emily quickly, defending Amanda. 'She's not all bad,' she added, remembering how Amanda had apologized to her. 'Not all of the time anyway. I bet she'll be back any minute.' She looked at the others. 'So, we're friends again?'

They grinned at each other. 'Friends,' they chorused.

'I think we should celebrate tonight by having some fun,' declared Molly. 'How about a pillow fight before bed?'

'Sounds cool to me,' agreed Tilda.

Molly grinned and rubbed her arms. 'Actually, I'm pretty cool out here right now. Let's go in and get warm!'

But just then, they heard someone calling them. Amanda was skating towards them with Madame Letsworth and

Madame Li. They were carrying blankets.

'Whatever's been going on?' Madame Letsworth demanded, looking at the ice monster sitting behind Alice.

They quickly explained.

Madame Letsworth smiled at the great bear. 'Thank you.'

He gave a soft growl, nuzzled Alice's hair and then dived into the water and disappeared under the ice.

Madame Li wrapped a blanket round Alice's shoulders. 'Come on, let's get you back inside and dry you off.'

As Alice stood up, there was the sound
of rustling in the bushes and a white face
with pricked ears popped out. 'It's
Prince!' gasped Alice.

Emily hurried to pick him up. The
puppy wriggled in her arms and licked
her nose. Everyone crowded round.

Madame Letsworth smiled. 'It looks
like everything's turned out well after all.'

'Got you!'
'No, got you!'
Emily ducked as Molly sent a pillow

flying at her head, but, as she turned, Tilda walloped her.

It was great fun. Eventually they collapsed on the beds, panting and laughing.

Emily felt very happy. No one was cross with anyone else any more. Tilda and Molly had promised to try and work better together and Alice, who was delighted that Prince had been found, had promised to practise more with Hannah. Even Amanda had changed. After tea, she had been really nice to Emily and asked her if she would like to add some more jumps to the routine.

Emily thought about the competition. It was only two days away. Who was going to win it? One thing was for sure, she couldn't wait to find out!

Chapter Nine
The Day of the Competition

The next two days raced by. On Sunday,
the day of the competition, everyone
woke up to find they had a costume
made by the frost fairies hanging at the
end of their bed.

'Oh, wow!' gasped Hannah as she held
up her costume – a magician's hat and
cloak to wear with a black-and-silver
skating dress.

'Aren't these cool?' said Alice, admiring what looked like an old-fashioned doll's outfit.

Molly and Tilda, who were dancing the story of Jack and Jill, had costumes straight out of a nursery-rhyme book. Tilda, who was Jill, had a dress with puffed sleeves and a short stripy skirt; Molly had knickerbockers and a matching stripy shirt and waistcoat.

Emily liked her prince costume too. She had black tights and a black tunic that had been embroidered with gold thread. A gold cloak was attached to her shoulders.

After breakfast, they all practised on the ice in their costumes and then at eleven o'clock the competition started.

It was brilliant watching everyone.

Heather and Zoe, who were in Ice Owls, did a fantastic routine, telling the story of the Ugly Duckling. It was obvious they had been working really hard; their movements were perfectly in time and neither of them made any mistakes. They kept the routine simple and it worked brilliantly.

Camilla and Olivia tried to do a very flashy, complicated routine showing the story of Sleeping Beauty, but they lost time with each other and Camilla fell

over. She looked furious.

Emily tried to hide her grin as they skated off to muted applause.

Hannah and Alice's magician and doll routine went very well until Alice lost track of what she was doing and ended up skating round in circles several times as she tried to remember what came next. She didn't seem to mind though and finished with a big smile and Hannah just grinned too.

Molly and Tilda's routine was full of energy, but half the time they didn't seem to have a clue what the other was doing. Still, they had everyone laughing as Molly pretended to fall over with the pail and then got up and dumped it on Tilda's head. It was definitely the funniest routine!

'It's our turn soon,' said Amanda to

Emily as Helena and Tess came on to the
ice.

Emily nodded. She felt nervous, but
she knew that all they could do was skate
their best. And they did. Amanda looked
beautiful in a costume made of white
feathers. She spun and jumped and Emily
tried her hardest to look like a prince in
love. She blocked everything else out and
focused on her skating. She managed her
four jumps perfectly and it was just great
to be out skating on the ice with
everyone watching.

Emily skated off feeling very happy.
She didn't think they were going to win
– Heather and Zoe's Ugly Duckling
routine had been much better than theirs
– but she'd really enjoyed performing in
front of everyone again.

'That was fun, wasn't it?' she said to Amanda as they came off the ice.

Amanda smiled. 'Yes, it was. I wish we could do it all over again!'

Finally the last pair skated and then the winners were announced.

'You all performed really, really well,' said Madame Letsworth, coming on to the ice with two pairs of violet skates with silver laces. 'But this was a competition to see how well you could skate with someone else and one pair stood out as a real team – Heather and Zoe. You've been practising well together all week and it really showed. Congratulations, girls.'

Everyone clapped as Heather and Zoe went on to the ice to collect the pretty violet skates. Heather was bright red and

looked very shy but absolutely delighted
as they took the skates and said thank
you. Emily felt really pleased for them.
Out of everyone, they were the pair who
really deserved to win.

When they skated off, Madame
Letsworth looked round at the girls.
'Now, before we finish, I'd just like to
mention another team effort. As I'm sure
all of you will have heard, there was an
incident a few days ago when Alice fell
into the river. I'd like to say a big well
done to the girls who showed great

bravery and acted as a real team that day to help her – Emily, Hannah, Molly, Tilda and Amanda. You might not have won the competition today, but you should all be proud of yourselves for the way you behaved.'

Emily and the others exchanged grins while everyone clapped.

'You're now free for the rest of the day,' Madame Letsworth said. 'And tomorrow, it's the beginning of a new week and the start of a new competition. I hope you've been listening in Madame Longley's lessons because next week you're going to be exploring outside the school and finding out a lot more about this land.'

'Wow! Sounds fun!' Hannah whispered to Emily, who nodded. It sounded brilliant!

★

'So, none of us won,' said Molly as they headed back to the common room a little later.

Emily smiled at her. 'Nope. But you know what? I don't mind.'

'I don't either,' said Molly. 'I'm just glad we're all friends again.'

'Me too,' said Hannah. 'That's much more important than winning a competition.'

Tilda and Alice came over. 'What are you guys going to do now?' Tilda asked.

'We don't have anything now until teatime.'

'I know!' said Emily. 'Let's go sledging.'

'Yeah, we can have races!' said Molly.

'And a snowball fight!' said Tilda, linking arms with her.

'Let's go!' said Hannah.

'Can I come too?' asked Amanda, sounding almost shy for once.

Emily smiled at her. 'Of course.'

Fifteen minutes later, they were all standing at the top of the slope in the garden with a sledge each.

'Get ready, everyone,' said Molly. 'When you get to the bottom, you have to run round the big tree over there, do a forward roll and then get back on your sledge. First one sitting down wins. OK?'

'OK,' they all chorused.

Emily took a deep breath of the clear, crisp air. The pale sun was shining and the snow lay in front of them like a thick, smooth blanket. She looked at the school and felt a wave of pure happiness. They were learning so many things, not just about skating but about everything.

And there's still so much more to learn, she thought. *We've still got to find out what the Ice Princess is going to have to do and how she will be chosen . . .*

A snowball hit her. She gasped and looked round. All the others were sitting on their sledges looking at her.

Molly, who had thrown the snowball, was grinning. 'Come on, Em – stop daydreaming!'

Emily giggled and sat down on her sledge too.

'One, two, three . . . go!' yelled Molly and, laughing and yelling, they whizzed away down the slope.

Do you dream of becoming an Ice Princess?

Have you ever wanted to go to a REAL Skating School?

All readers of *Skating School* get FREE membership to the National Ice Skating Association's Skate UK programme!

Skate UK will help you to learn all the moves and basic skills you need to become a true Ice Princess! It's all about fun and continuous movement and is taught in groups, so why not share your love of *Skating School* with your friends and bring them too?

To get your free membership, go to
www.iceskating.org.uk/skatingschool
and enter the secret password: **Twirl**.

Skate UK is taught by licensed NISA coaches and can be assisted by trained Programme Assistants.

For full terms and conditions visit:
www.lindachapman.co.uk
www.iceskating.org.uk/skatingschool

Design your own ice-skating dress!

The tiny frost fairies have been working overtime designing the beautiful dresses for the girls to wear in the Ice-skating Academy competitions.

Using this dress as a template, the fairies need you to draw the most magical ice-skating outfit you can think of. Every month one lucky winner will receive a magical *Skating School* goody bag!

Send your drawing

with your name and address to:

Skating School Competition, Puffin Marketing, 80 Strand, London WC2R 0RL

Or e-mail them to: **skatingschool@uk.penguingroup.com**

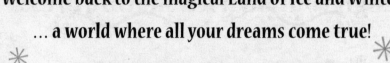

Welcome back to the magical Land of Ice and Winter
… a world where all your dreams come true!

A brand-new
Skating School series

Coming soon!

Hi there,

I hope you've enjoyed reading about the adventures of the girls who go to the Magic Ice-skating Academy. I love writing them all down! Wouldn't it be amazing to go to the Land of Ice and Winter and see all the creatures who live there? Can you imagine holding an actual ice dragon or talking to a frost fairy?

Sometimes readers write to me and ask about my life. Being a writer is the best job ever. I live in a cottage in a village with my family and two dogs – a Bernese mountain dog and a golden retriever. I spend my days writing and going to visit schools and libraries to talk about writing.

I always think I'm really lucky because I get to spend my days writing about magic – mermaids, unicorns, stardust spirits, genies and now the Land of Ice and Winter. If you love them too then why not go to **www.lindachapman.co.uk** and join the Sparkle Club? It's my online fan club with loads of activities and downloads, and you can only get to it by using the secret password at the back of this book. Have fun!

Love,

Linda
xxx